Hans Christian Andersen

Fairy Tale Classics

Illustrated by
Yuri Salzman

Published in the United States and Canada by
Joshua Morris Publishing, Inc.
221 Danbury Road
Wilton, Connecticut 06897

Printed in Hong Kong

Contents

The Emperor's New Clothes

Many years ago there was an Emperor who loved beautiful new clothes so much that he spent all his time and his money on being splendidly dressed. Nothing interested him more than an occasion to appear in his finest attire. In fact, he spent far more time admiring himself in the mirror than he did running his country. He had a suit for every hour of the day, and just as it might be said of a King, "He is in his Council," it was always said of this one that, "The Emperor is in his wardrobe."

9

A celebration in honor of the Emperor was to be held in a week. He was to lead a procession through the town. All the people would line the streets to look at him. And this made the Emperor very upset for he had no new clothes to wear. Yet, one afternoon, two crafty strangers, pretending to be weavers and tailors, came to town. Insisting that they could weave the finest cloth the Emperor had ever seen, they demanded to see him. Indeed, the Emperor could not resist their tempting offer, and as he was desperate for new clothes for his appearance, he invited them to his court.

"Your Majesty," they said, bowing respectfully. "Your taste in clothes is magnificent, your dress is unsurpassed, but we have something to offer you which will put your other clothes to shame."

"And what could that be?" the Emperor asked haughtily, for his clothiers had searched the world for his finery.

"We can weave the most wonderful material imaginable," said one excitedly. "Not only are the colors beautiful and the patterns unique, but the cloth is actually magic!"

"Magic?" the Emperor scoffed in an arrogant voice. But, his curiosity was getting the better of him. "Go on," he said.

"This cloth, Your Grace," the second man continued, "will be invisible to anyone who is unfit for

his position or anyone who is a fool. Only those who are well worth their work and those who are wise will be able to see the extraordinary suit."

"This would be a wonderful suit to own," exclaimed the Emperor. "By wearing it," he said gleefully, "I will discover who is fit for their position in my palace and who is a fool. And, of course, I will make the most marvelous appearance of my life. I will wear the suit in the next grand procession!" So he gave the cunning swindlers a great deal of money in order for them to begin their work at once. And so they did.

11

The two thieves were given a special room in the palace. They requested exquisite silks and fine gold threads, but kept everything for themselves. Then, they set up two looms and pretended to weave what was actually nothing at all.

Consumed with curiosity, the Emperor thought, "I would love to see my new cloth." However, he was a bit nervous. He decided to let his trusted Minister have the first look.

So off went the Minister to visit the two swindlers who were working busily at their empty looms. "My goodness!" thought the Minister staring as hard as he could. "What is the meaning of this? I cannot see a thing!" But he said nothing.

The thieves invited the Minister to step closer to the loom. "Aren't the colors wonderful?" they asked. "Do you see the beauty of the design?" Graciously they pointed to the empty looms and the poor Minister looked and looked but he could not see a single thread, for, in truth, there was none.

"Am I a fool? Can it be that I am unfit for my position?" he asked himself. "Certainly not. But, whatever the reason, no one will ever know that I cannot see this cloth!"

"Have you nothing to say?" the weavers asked.

"Oh, why, the material is stunning," said the poor Minister peering through his glasses. "I will report to the Emperor that I am most satisfied!"

The Emperor could hardly wait to see his suit after hearing the Minister's praises. On the day of the grand procession, the two thieves went into the Emperor's chambers pretending to carry something incredibly delicate. "Here are your clothes, Your Majesty! They are as light as a feather. Truly you will feel as if you have nothing on at all."

Slowly the two swindlers helped the Emperor put on each piece of his new suit. When the Emperor was supposedly dressed, he searched the mirror for a glimpse of his splendid new suit but, in fact, he saw nothing at all.

Nevertheless, he strode confidently in front of the grand procession. All the people gathered in the streets and leaned out their windows. Naturally, no one would admit that they could not see his clothes, for that would reveal him to be either a fool or unfit for his position.

Suddenly, a boy cried, "But he has nothing on!"

"Listen to the voice of innocence!" said the child's father, and the boy's words were whispered from one to the other.

"He has nothing on!" everyone finally shouted. And the Emperor, aghast, knew that they must be right. But he held his head high and walked proudly for he knew the parade must continue. Behind him, his servants followed faithfully, holding the train of the robe, that indeed, was not there at all.

The Flying Trunk

There was once a merchant who was so rich that he could have paved an entire street with silver and gold. But he used his money wisely and, for every quarter he spent, he received a dollar in return. Thus, he built his fortune until he died.

His son inherited all his money and led a merry life with no thought of saving. So, it was not long before he was left with nothing but a pair of worn slippers and an old-fashioned dressing gown. His friends did not want to be seen with him, but one, kinder than the others, sent him a trunk with this note: "It is best for you to pack your belongings and leave." Since he had nothing to pack, he climbed into the trunk himself.

And what a surprise! As soon as he was in the trunk, it took off into the air. Up it went, high above the clouds and far away. The trunk sailed along breezily until it came down in the land of the Turks. There he hid his trunk in the woods and walked into town, where he found everyone outfitted as he was—in a long dressing gown and slippers. He did not look like a poor stranger at all.

A great castle with a window high up in a tower caught his eye. "Who lives there?" he wondered, and so he asked a woman who was passing by.

"The King's beautiful daughter," the old woman replied. "It is foretold that she will be unhappy when she falls in love so no one is permitted to visit her without her mother and father being present."

"We'll see," said the merchant's son and he went back into the woods, climbed into his trunk, flew directly to the roof of the Princess' tower and crept into her window.

The Princess, who was fast asleep, was so lovely that he could not help stealing one kiss from her. When she awoke with a start, he convinced her that he was a Turkish god who had come down from the sky to marry her. She was flattered, indeed, and so they sat down side by side and he told her charming tales that melted her heart. When he finally proposed to her, she agreed lovingly.

"You must come here on Saturday when the King and Queen are here," she said. "Please tell them a delightful story that is both moral and funny. My parents are especially fond of a good story so they will surely let us marry if you can do this."

"Very well," the merchant's son answered. "I will bring no other present than a fine story." And he spent the next few days in the woods carefully preparing what he would say.

On Saturday, the King and Queen greeted the merchant's son cordially and then asked eagerly for his story. He began immediately:

"Once there was a bundle of matches who lived in a kitchen. They believed themselves to be very important and were proud of their noble origin from a fir tree. 'We provide light and fire,' they boasted, 'and nothing can be done without us.'

'My life is very different,' said the heavy iron pot. 'From the beginning, I have been scrubbed, boiled and burned, but I know that I am needed.'

'Let's not talk about ourselves,' said the sugar bowl. 'I'll tell a story. I spent my childhood...,' and she went on and on until everyone was so tired of listening that they all began to interrupt.

'Let me dance,' cried the pewter tongs as she began a spritely whirl.

And then the teapot began to sing.

The market basket was disgusted with everyone. 'Why, all you care about is your own importance. Why don't we all clear up this messy kitchen?'

'Yes, good idea,' they all agreed, but everyone kept on thinking how superior each was to the other.

Just then the maid came in and they all were very still. Taking the matches, she lit a fire.

'There,' thought the matches, 'now they will see who is the most brilliant here!' And then the match burned out."

"What a delightful story!" exclaimed the King and Queen. "Yes, you shall marry our daughter."

On the evening before the wedding, the entire city rejoiced. Crowds gathered in the squares, delicious foods were shared, and the people whistled and sang with joy.

Wanting to do something to add to the merry-making, the merchant's son bought fireworks of all kinds and flew up into the sky in his magic trunk.

Whizz! Crackle! Boom! The firecrackers and rockets exploded into the most glorious display of color and light. The Turks could hardly believe their eyes. This convinced them that their Princess was, indeed, marrying a god.

When the merchant's son returned, he went into town, anxious to hear what the people were saying.

"I saw the god myself," declared many a man. "He had eyes like flashing stars!" How proud the merchant's son was to hear such wonderful things about himself!

Yet, when he returned to the woods, he found that his trunk had burnt to ashes—probably from the spark of a firecracker. So, he could never fly to his bride nor prove himself to be a god ever again.

All day long the Princess waited for him on the roof of the palace. She waits for him still. And he roams the world telling stories, but none so charming as the one about the proud matches.

The Ugly Duckling

It was a glorious summer day in the country. Flowers bloomed across the meadow down to the lake. Near the edge of the water, a duck was sitting on her nest, waiting impatiently for her eggs to hatch. She had been there such a long time!

At last the eggs began to crack. "Peep! Peep!" the tiny ducklings cried as they pecked their way through the shells and into the world. "Peep! Peep!"

The mother duck looked about eagerly. "Finally you are all here," she said, very much relieved. But then she noticed that the biggest egg of all had not hatched. "How much longer can it possibly take?" she sighed.

Soon, an old duck waddled by for a visit and asked, "How are you doing?"

"Wonderfully! Aren't my ducklings beautiful?" said the mother duck proudly. "Yet, this last one is taking so long to hatch."

"Why that's not your egg," said the old duck smugly. "I'll bet that's a turkey's egg. I was once fooled myself and had no end of trouble. I'd leave it and go worry about your adorable ducklings."

"I can't do that," answered the mother duck. "A little more time will make the difference."

Very soon after the big egg did crack. And out tumbled the newborn, a mess of feathers and fluff. "My," thought the mother duck, "you certainly are ugly; not at all like the others!" The ducklings noticed too, and did not like him one bit. But all their mother said was, "All right! Into the water with all of you and we'll see if you can swim."

"Quack, quack," she called and in went the ducklings, even the ugly one. They disappeared beneath the water for a moment, but popped right up and were soon swimming about.

"Well, at least he's a good swimmer," the mother duck thought as she watched the ugly duckling, "but he sure is a strange duck!"

The ducklings were splashing and playing and having a wonderful time, all except the ugly duckling. His brothers and sisters pushed and shoved him, tweaked his beak and made fun of him. It was hopeless to try and join in their games.

"Leave him alone," the mother duck warned as she came out of the lake and shook off her feathers. "Time to get out of the water and be introduced to the members of the barnyard. Stay close to me, walk with your legs apart, and watch out for the cat! Oh, yes, and bow to the eldest duck, for she is the most important of all!"

But no sooner had their little procession entered the barnyard than the other ducks and animals began to complain. "Look at that ugly duckling! He's just too...unsightly!"

"What an embarrassment! He'll never fit in with the rest of us."

"I just won't look at him."

When they stood before the eldest duck, she said to the mother, "Your children are lovely except for *that* one. It's such a shame."

As the rest of the ducklings made themselves at home in the barnyard, the poor ugly one was bitten and pinched by the ducks and hens. He was terrified by the turkey cock who puffed himself up, fanned his feathers out like sails and ran straight at the duckling, gobbling and flapping his wings. Even the girl who fed the animals pushed him aside when she came to the barnyard.

Things soon grew worse. Everyone chased the unhappy duckling, his sisters and brothers teased him, and even his mother said, "How I wish you were...different!"

The ugly duckling was so miserable that one day he slipped through the fence and just kept running and running.

Eventually, he found himself in a marsh where, tired and miserable, he fell asleep. The next morning he was awakened by the quacking of some wild ducks who lived there. "What kind of duck are you?" they asked. "You're so ugly!" Not waiting for an answer, they flew quickly away, arching high across the sky. As the sad duckling watched them, he wished so much to be one of them. But, all of a sudden, there was a loud bang! The frightened little duck hid in the reeds. Soon, some large dogs with big white teeth came by. There were hunters too! But they laughed at him and the dogs would not even sniff him.

"No one will ever like me," he thought.

That night, the duckling left the marsh, wandering far from home. Finally he came to a small hut. The door was ajar, so he crept inside. An old woman lived there with her cat and her hen.

In the morning, the cat and the hen discovered the intruder. The old woman, who couldn't see well, eventually saw the ugly duckling too. "What have we here?" she said. "A nice fat duckling, and maybe some duck eggs too, if we're lucky!"

But the cat did not like sharing his home with the ugly duckling. "You can't even arch your back and purr," said the cat while showing his claws.

Then the hen scolded him. "If you aren't going to lay any eggs, what good are you?" she demanded.

The duckling was miserable. Longing to find some place where he would be loved, he fled back into the wide world.

The sad, ugly duckling spent many days on his own. Soon it was autumn—and the evenings were growing cold. But the duckling had found a quiet lake where he spent his time swimming, each day more expertly. One evening, during a glorious sunset, a whole flock of magnificent birds flew out of the bushes. The duckling had never seen anything so beautiful. They were white swans, with graceful necks. Spreading their wings, they flew up high in the air. Through the long winter that eventually came, he dreamed of those birds.

That winter was unusually cold. The duckling searched for food and swam to keep warm. Exhausted at last, he could no longer keep his legs moving. The ice froze about him. Luckily, a kind farmer discovered the duckling, broke the ice with his axe and brought the poor creature home.

In the warm house, the duckling revived. The farmer's children tried to play with him, but he was frightened. Flapping his wings, he knocked over a pitcher and splashed milk everywhere. The children came after him and so he flew higher to get away. Then, being so tired of trying to escape, the duckling fell into a tub of butter. While struggling out of the butter, he then tumbled into a barrel of flour. The farmer's wife shrieked! The children laughed noisily. He was so terrified, he flew out the open door, back into the snow.

It would be too sad to tell about the long, harsh winter the duckling had to endure. He stayed in the marshes until, finally, it was spring.

The duckling stretched his wings and found them to be more powerful than before. He beat the air vigorously and before he knew it, he had flown into a beautiful garden. Straight before him was a lake with three swans gliding over the water. The duckling recognized these splendid birds and a strange sadness came over him.

"I must go to visit them," he said to himself. "It doesn't matter if they peck me and tease me. Better to be pecked by them than the hens in the barnyard or to spend another winter alone."

So he flew onto the lake and swam toward the swans. Bowing his head, the poor creature said, "Go ahead. Say how ugly I am." But not one of the birds said a word. They just swam about him happily. Then, he happened to glance at his reflection in the water. He saw not an ugly duckling, but a beautiful white swan. *He* was a swan himself!

The swans circled him and stroked him with their bills. Some children came to the lake and threw bread into the water. "Oh, look!" they shouted. "A new swan and it's the prettiest of all!"

Then he raised his slender neck and rejoiced, feeling the happiness he never dreamed would be possible for an ugly duckling.

The Princess and the Pea

Once there was a Prince who wanted to marry. But, of course, the Prince would only marry a real Princess. That was not an easy task. He traveled great distances and searched far and wide, but he could never be absolutely sure that the Princesses he met were real. Finally, he returned to his home, sad and discouraged. He had given up hope that he would ever find the Princess of his dreams.

Yet, one night not long after his return to the castle, there was a terrible storm. Thunder and lightning crackled in the sky, and heavy rains soaked the earth. All of a sudden, someone came knocking at the door. The King and Queen rushed to see who it could be.

A pretty, young girl stood in the doorway, wet and bedraggled. Her hair clung to her neck and her clothes dripped with raindrops. Streams of water trickled down into a puddle all around her. She said, to the King and Queen's astonishment, that she was a *real* Princess.

"We'll soon see about that!" thought the Queen, but she gave no hint of what she was about to do.

After letting the poor girl in, and seating her by the hearth in the kitchen, the Queen marched directly to the bedroom. There, she stripped the bed down to its frame, taking off the sheets and quilts and even the mattress. She placed a pea on the top of the wooden frame, right in the very center.

Then the Queen ordered her servants to lay twenty mattresses on top of the pea. On top of that, they laid twenty feather quilts. And that is where the Princess spent the night, on top of the pea, twenty mattresses and twenty quilts.

The next morning they asked her if she had slept well and comfortably.

"No, I slept just horribly!" the Princess replied. "I hardly closed my eyes the entire night. There is something in that bed that is so hard that I am black and blue all over. It was simply dreadful!"

The King and Queen were ecstatic. It was clear that the young woman was a real Princess. Who else could have felt the pea through twenty mattresses and twenty quilts! No one had such delicate feelings but a real Princess.

The Prince was convinced. Happy that he had found a real Princess at last, he made her his wife. And, of course, they lived happily ever after. The pea is placed in a museum where it can still be seen, if no one has taken it.

And that is a true story.

The Shepherdess and the Chimney Sweep

Have you ever seen an antique wooden cabinet that is carved with curious figures, flowers and animals? Well, just such a cabinet stood in a parlor in the home of a wealthy dowager. In the middle of the cabinet was a tiny figure—a man with legs like a goat, horns on his head and a terrible, evil grin. He was called Field-Marshall-Major-General-Billy-Goat's-Legs. Who knows why he was ever carved on that cabinet but, there he was, always staring across at a long mahogany table.

On the table stood a pretty little shepherdess made of porcelain and glittering with touches of gold.

Quite close to her stood a chimney sweep, black with coal, yet his face was clean and fair. He and the shepherdess were very much in love.

Near them was another figure, much larger and made of porcelain too. He was an old Chinaman who could nod his head. He claimed he was the shepherdess' grandfather and that she could only do as he said. So, when Field-Marshall-Major-General-Billy-Goat's-Legs asked to marry the shepherdess, the Chinaman nodded his head in agreement.

"I won't go into that dark cabinet," cried the shepherdess. "I have heard he has eleven wives in there already."

"Then you shall be the twelfth," the Chinaman answered. "Tonight you shall be married." Then he nodded his head and fell asleep.

The shepherdess wept and said to her beloved chimney sweep, "We cannot stay here. Will you go with me into the wide world?"

"Whatever you wish," he replied. And he helped her down from the table. When they reached the floor, they could see that the Field-Marshall was in an uproar. The shepherdess was to be his wife and she was eloping with the chimney sweep. He shouted to the Chinaman, "They are running away! Stop them!" And he stamped his cloven hooves and grinned his evil grin.

The two were so frightened that they hid inside an open drawer under a windowsill. There, a tiny puppet show was in progress. The audience was four packs of cards, not quite complete. They sat in rows intently watching the story of two lovers who were being kept apart. The little shepherdess could not help crying. It was just like her own story.

"I cannot bear this," she sobbed. "We must leave the drawer." But when they were back on the floor, they saw the Chinaman shaking with rage and the shepherdess nearly fainted with fear.

But the brave chimney sweep took her by the hand and ran to the fireplace. "Do you really have the courage to go into the wide world?" he asked. "Do you realize that we may never return?"

"Yes, I do," she replied tearfully.

So he led her up the chimney where it was dark as could be. But just when it became pitch black and the shepherdess was terrified, the chimney sweep shouted, "Look, a shining star!" And the light from a beautiful star shone into the chimney. They struggled up higher and higher, clinging to the steep walls. The chimney sweep helped the shepherdess and supported her until, at last, they climbed out and sat down, so very tired.

The immense star-lit sky sparkled above them and the roofs of the houses in the town filled the distance below. The world was much larger than the shepherdess had expected. "This is too much," she cried. "I cannot bear a world as overwhelming as this. How I wish I were safe, back on our table. I'm sorry. I just did not know what the world was like. Please, if you love me, take me back."

The chimney sweep tried to make her listen to reason and reminded her of the terrible Field-Marshall, but she pleaded and kissed him so lovingly that he could not refuse, foolish as it was. So with a great deal of difficulty, they climbed back down through the chimney and into the fireplace.

It was very quiet. Timidly, the two peeked out into the room. Alas! The poor Chinaman, when he had tried to come after them, had fallen on the floor and had broken into two pieces.

"How awful!" cried the shepherdess. "And it is all my fault. I shall never forgive myself."

"Be patient," said the chimney sweep. "He can be put back together with some glue and a post in his back. He will be as good as new and just as before." Slowly, they climbed up the table and took their old places next to each other. "It does not seem like we have come very far for all our trouble," the chimney sweep sighed. He wished that somehow their lives would be changed.

The next morning, the Chinaman was put back together, but with the post in his back, he could no longer nod his head. However, the chimney sweep and shepherdess did not know that.

"You have a very proud look since your accident," Field-Marshall-Major-General-Billy-Goat's-Legs told the Chinaman angrily. "Well, am I to have the shepherdess or not?" he demanded.

The shepherdess and the chimney sweep looked at the old Chinaman fearfully, for they were afraid he might nod. But he could not.

So the two porcelain figures stood side by side and loved each other until the end of their days, when they were broken in pieces.

47

The Tinderbox

A soldier wearing a sword and carrying a knapsack came marching down the road. "One, two! One, two!" he said with each step he took. Along the way, he met a witch who was terribly ugly.

"Good evening," she said. "You look like a fine soldier and an honest man. How would you like to have all the money you could ever want?"

"Very much, indeed," replied the startled soldier.

"Do you see that tree," she said while pointing a long and bony finger. "It's hollow inside. There is an entrance near the top. If I tie a rope around your waist, you can slide to the bottom and then I can hoist you up again."

"But, why?" asked the soldier.

"To get money, of course," said the witch. "At the bottom you will find a long passage lit by hundreds of candles. There will be three doors, each with its own key. In the first room, you will see a large chest with a dog sitting on it whose eyes are as big as teacups. But don't worry about him. I'll lend you my blue-checked apron. Just grab hold of him quickly and get him to sit on the apron. The

chest is filled with copper coins. Take as many as you please, but if you prefer silver, go to the next room. There you will find another chest filled with silver and a dog whose eyes are as big as mill wheels. But don't worry about him. Get him to sit on the apron and take what you wish, unless you'd rather have gold. In the third room, there is a chest with a dog whose eyes are as huge as towers. But don't worry. Get him on the apron and fill your knapsack with gold."

"I will go," said the soldier, "but what do you want in return?"

"Not one coin," said the witch. "Just bring me the tinderbox which my grandmother left there."

"Very well," replied the soldier. Down he went into the tree and, just as the witch had said, he found himself in a passage lit by hundreds of candles. He opened the first door and gasped at the sight of the dog with eyes as big as teacups staring at him.

"Good boy," said the soldier as he sat him on the witch's apron and immediately filled his pockets with copper coins. Then he went on to the next room. Ugh! There sat a dog with eyes as big as mill wheels but the soldier didn't hesitate. He put the dog on the blue-checked cloth and opened the chest. Flinging away the copper, he filled his pockets and his knapsack with silver. Then he went into the third room and what did he see? An enormous dog with eyes as big as towers staring at him. Fearlessly, he made the dog sit on the witch's apron. Just as the witch had promised, the third chest contained nothing but glittering gold! So the soldier threw away all his silver coins and stuffed his pockets, his knapsack, his cap and boots so full of gold that he could barely walk. He shut the chest, closed the door and shouted to the witch to hoist him up.

"Do you have the tinderbox?" she asked.

"I've forgotten!" he exclaimed and went back for it. Then the witch pulled him up. "What do you want the tinderbox for?" he asked.

"None of your business," she answered sharply.

"Tell me or I'll cut off your head," he said.

"No!" cried the witch.

So the soldier cut off her head. And taking the tinderbox, he headed for town.

Once there be began to spend his fortune. He dressed in the highest fashion, went to the theater and royal gardens and gave money to the poor. Since he was now a fine gentleman, he had many friends. Eventually he heard of the princess who lived in a great castle high above the town. The king permitted no one to see her because it had been foretold that she would marry a common soldier. He wished that he could see her, but he was never allowed.

And so he went on, thoughtlessly spending money until his pockets were empty.

One evening, when he did not even have a coin for a candle, he remembered the tinderbox and in it he found the stump of a candle. No sooner had he struck the box three times for a light than the dog with eyes as big as towers burst into his room and said, "What does my lord command?"

"What a marvelous tinderbox, indeed!" exclaimed the soldier. "Bring me some money!" he yelled. And the dog did. It did not take long for the soldier to understand the magical powers of his tinderbox. At one, two or three strikes, one of the dogs appeared to do his bidding.

One night, the soldier was thinking about the Princess. Taking his tinderbox, he struck the box three times and immediately the dog with eyes as

big as towers appeared. "I wish to see the Princess," he declared. In an instant the dog returned with the Princess on his back. She was truly beautiful. The soldier bent down and kissed her. Then, the dog took off, returning the Princess to the castle.

But a bag of flour with a tiny hole in it had been tied to the Princess' waist. Flour had seeped out, leaving a trail from the castle to the soldier's door. In the morning, the Princess told the King and Queen of a strange dream of being carried away by a dog and kissed by a soldier. Immediately, the King followed the path of flour to the soldier's home and threw him in prison.

The soldier was to be hanged the next day. What could he do? He had carelessly left his tinder-box in his room. In the morning, from his barred window, he saw a young boy go by. He shouted to him, "Run to my room and get my tinder-box and I'll pay you well." Eager for the money, the boy brought the tinderbox. And this is what happened next.

Hundreds of people, the King and Queen, the judges and all the councilors were gathered at the gallows. When the time came for the hanging, the soldier stood calmly. When the rope was finally put around his neck, he called out, "As my last request, please let me smoke a pipe of tobacco."

The King could not refuse. So the soldier took out his tinderbox and struck a light, once, then twice, then three times, and in a flash the dog with the eyes of teacups, the dog with the eyes of mill wheels and the dog with the eyes of towers stood at his command.

"Help me!" the soldier cried.

The terrifying dogs dashed at the judge and the councilors and even the King and Queen and tossed them high into the air. The crowd, frightened and amazed, shouted, "Good soldier, be our King and the Princess shall be your Queen!"

And so it was. There was a great wedding feast. And the three dogs came and stared at everyone with their huge, strange eyes.

The Little Fir Tree

Far away in the deep forest there grew a pretty little fir tree. Although the sun shone and the air was fresh, the fir tree was not happy, not at all. He wished so much to be tall like the older trees that he never noticed the warm sun and gentle breezes. He never enjoyed the children who came to the forest to fill their baskets with berries. And when the boys and girls sat down near the little tree and said, "Oh, what a pretty little tree," he was even more unhappy than before.

"If only I were as tall as the other trees," complained the little fir tree. "Birds would build nests in my branches and I would be able to see the wide world. When the wind blew, I would bow proudly, just like the others!'' The fir tree was so concerned with himself that he never took pleasure in the sunsets or songbirds, or the beautiful clouds overhead.

Sometimes, in the winter, when the forest was covered with sparkling snow, a rabbit would go by and jump as high as the little fir tree's middle branches. How awful he felt, to be nearly as high as a rabbit's hop!

In the autumn, woodcutters arrived to cut down the largest trees. The fir tree shuddered when he heard the great trees crash to the ground. After the men collected a cart load, the trees were stripped of their branches and taken from the forest.

"They must be very important trees for people to want to take them away," the little fir tree thought. "I wonder what they will become?"

One day, when the woodcutters were in the forest, a stork visited the little fir tree. "I have flown over every sea to Egypt and back. I have seen such trees on the masts of tall sailing ships," he said.

"Oh, how I wish I were tall enough to go to sea," the little fir tree sighed when the stork flew away.

"Enjoy what you are," answered the sun and the wind. And they caressed the little fir tree with warm sunlight and gentle breezes, but he would not be comforted at all.

When Christmas drew near, many trees, some not much taller than the little fir tree, were cut down and loaded onto carts. Their branches were not removed for these trees were selected for their beauty. The fir tree wondered, "Why were they chosen? Where are they going? What will they become?"

"We know, we know," sang the sparrows. "In town, we peek in the windows of the houses and we have seen them in beautiful rooms dressed in the most splendid manner. Exquisite decorations are

hung from their branches. And the trees glow from the light of hundreds of candles."

"And then what?" asked the fir tree breathless with longing. But the sparrows knew no more.

The next year the fir tree yearned for Christmas, for he knew that something wonderful must happen to a tree who is so honored. The warm sun and soft breezes tried to make him happy where he was, but he cared nothing for his surroundings.

The fir tree grew a bit taller by next winter and so, when Christmas finally came near, he was one of the trees to be taken from the forest. He felt so proud being carried away in a handsome cart.

Eventually the fir tree was delivered to a large

house. His trunk was placed in a tub of sand and covered with a lovely green and red cloth. Then, the tree was decorated with sugarplums, candied apples, toys, sweets and tiny candles. A large gold star was fastened like a crown to his very top. "What is going to happen next?" thought the trembling tree, for he longed for still greater things to come.

That evening, the candles were lit and the tree was magnificent. "A story, a story," the children cried to a man who came forward gladly.

"It shall be Humpty Dumpty," he said as the children gathered around him. And he told the story of Humpty Dumpty who fell down the stairs but recovered and married a beautiful princess.

63

"So that is what happens in the world," thought the tree. "Someday I shall marry a princess."

When the story was finished the children opened all the presents and ate most of the candy from the tree. Everyone had said that it was the most beautiful Christmas tree that had ever been. The little fir tree thought this was one of the happiest days of his life.

The next morning the tree was taken to the attic and left among some dusty boxes and forgotten trunks. There he waited day after day for something new to happen, something greater than had ever happened before.

Suddenly, he heard, "Squeek, squeek," and discovered several mice scurrying among his branches.

"Where did you come from?" they asked.

"Before I was brought here, I lived in the forest." And he told them all about the warm sun and soft breezes and the kind birds.

"How happy you must have been," said the mice.

"Happy?" the fir tree replied in surprise. "Yes, I suppose those were the good times," he said. And he went on to tell them all about Christmas Eve when he had been adorned with presents and candles.

"Oh, how happy, you must have been then, old fir tree," exclaimed the mice.

"Old? I'm not old at all!" the tree exclaimed. "I am still young and in the spring, perhaps, I will marry a princess like Humpty Dumpty."

"Who is Humpty Dumpty?" they asked. So he told them the story and the mice were delighted.

Soon the mice stopped visiting. The fir tree became lonely. "But," he thought, "I will be happy when they take me out of this terrible attic."

And before long, they did drag him roughly down the stairs, out of the house and into the garden. There, he felt the warm sun again and the gentle breezes and saw that everything was fresh and blooming. "Now I shall live!" cried the tree joyfully and he tried to spread out his branches. But they were yellow and withered with no life in them.

The children who were playing in the garden were the very children who had cherished him at Christmas. And yet, one child came running up to the fir tree and took the gold star crown from his top.

The tree thought about his young days in the forest, of the wonderful Christmas and of the mice who had listened to his stories and remembrances. "If only I had been happy where I was—in the forest with the sun shining and the cool breezes," he sighed. "Now it is too late. It is all past." And then a man came and chopped the fir tree into logs and placed them in a bonfire.

The children chased around the fire and sounded just like they did on one of the happiest days of the fir tree's life. But that is all past, just as this story is past, for even stories must come to an end.

The Nightingale

In China, as you may know, the Emperor is Chinese and so are all the people. This story is true and took place in that faraway land a long time ago. And it is a story well worth remembering.

The Emperor of China lived in the most splendid palace in the world. It was made of the finest porcelain, so fragile that one could hardly touch it. The garden was filled with colorful flowers, fastened with tinkling silver bells so that no one could pass by without taking notice of their exquisite beauty. Who would ever want to leave such a place? Certainly the Emperor never did. All the beauty of the world seemed to be right within his palace.

Beyond the garden was a forest of tall trees which grew right down to the sea. Among its branches lived a nightingale whose song was so sweet that even the poor fishermen would stop their work just to listen. People traveled from all over the world to see the Emperor's great city, but what they remembered most was the nightingale. And when they wrote books about their visit, they saved their highest praise for the little bird.

One day the Emperor discovered one of these books. He had never known about this nightingale. Angrily, he summoned his Chief Courtier. "Why has this remarkable nightingale never been brought to my attention?" the Emperor demanded. "It is my wish that the bird sing in my court tonight. If it is not found, the entire court will be punished."

"I shall find it," said the Chief Courtier, but he had never heard of the nightingale either, and had no idea where to look. Not wishing to be punished, the entire court joined in the search, racing frantically all over the palace and the garden.

At last, they discovered a little kitchen maid who said, "Of course, I know the nightingale. Every night on my way home through the forest I hear its sweet song."

So the girl took the Chief Courtier into the woods. Unaccustomed to the outdoors as he was, he heard a frog croaking and thought that was the nightingale. Then he heard a cow mooing, and thought that was the nightingale. But, at last, the maid exclaimed, "That's it! There, in the branches. Just listen!"

"But it's just an ordinary black bird," commented the Chief Courtier.

"Dear nightingale," said the kitchen maid, "our Emperor wishes you would sing for him tonight."

"My song sounds best out here," said the bird, "but I'll be happy to please the Emperor."

The palace was decorated for the arrival of the nightingale. The walls of porcelain were polished and the magnificent flowers with their tinkling bells filled the rooms. The entire court gathered and even the little kitchen maid—who was now an Imperial Cook—was allowed to stand among the courtiers.

A golden perch for the nightingale was placed in the great hall right next to the throne of the Emperor. The nightingale sang so sweetly, so mellifluously, that tears welled in the Emperor's eyes and eventually rolled down his cheeks. With each song, the nightingale sang even more beautifully.

"The nightingale," said the Emperor, "must have a golden scarf for its neck." But the bird refused.

"No, I have been rewarded enough," the bird replied. "I have seen tears in the Emperor's eyes, and they have wondrous power." And then the nightingale sang again, more gloriously than ever.

It was decreed that the nightingale should remain at court and have its own golden cage. It was free to fly out twice a day and once at night—yet only with long silk ribbons attached to each of its legs so the nightingale could not fly away.

One day, a gift from the Emperor of Japan arrived at the palace. It was a golden, mechanical nightingale, decorated with precious jewels. When it was wound up, the artificial bird sang one of the very songs that the real nightingale sang.

"How lovely," everyone gasped when the mechanical bird sang at court. "Now the two must sing together." So the two birds sang, but each had its own way, so they did not complement one another. The music master defended the jeweled bird, insisting that it kept perfect time, just the way he taught music. And so the artificial bird sang again alone—exactly the same tune, thirty-three times. Everyone was so captivated that they failed to notice that the real nightingale had flown out the window.

The music master assured the Emperor that he had lost nothing. After all, with the artificial bird, everything was definite, so one always knew what to expect. Besides, its mechanical parts were a perfect example of human genius. The real nightingale was banished from the empire.

The artificial bird was revered by all. People came from far and wide just to hear its song. After a year, everyone knew the song by heart and enjoyed it all the more because they could sing along.

But one evening, while the mechanical bird was singing, there was a sudden snap, and while the mechanisms seemed to be whirring along, no sound came out. Alarmed, the Emperor called for his watchmaker. Although he was able to put the bird back together, he said that all the gears and parts were so worn that the bird should not sing more than once a year.

Five years passed and, although the mechanical bird sang each year, sorrow filled the land. The Emperor was very sick and not expected to live. Cold and pale, he lay in his great bed.

"Music, music," he cried to his golden bird, hoping a song could ease the pain. But the bird just lay quiet while the Emperor's life grew dim.

Just then, the most magnificent song came from outside the Emperor's window. It was the real nightingale who had heard that the Emperor was ailing and came to sing to him of comfort and hope. As the sweet music filled the room, the Emperor became stronger.

"Thank you," sighed the Emperor with tears in his eyes. "I sent you away and you have returned to save me. How can I repay you?"

"You have repaid me," replied the bird, "for I received your tears, more precious than any jewels."

"You will stay in the palace with me forever," the Emperor cried.

"No," answered the nightingale. "But I will come to you every night and sing by your window so you can be happy and well. I will sing of all that happens in your empire, but you must promise me one thing. Tell no one that a little bird tells you everything." And he flew away.

That same day a celebration was held, for everyone was happy to see their Emperor well.

The Swineherd

There once was a Prince who was not as wealthy as we imagine Princes to be. Still, the fortunes of his kingdom would permit him to marry well. Although there were many Princesses who wished to be his bride, he wanted only the daughter of an Emperor who lived in a nearby valley.

It so happened that a rare and lovely rosebush grew near his palace. A single rose bloomed there only once in five years, but it's fragrance was so sweet that anyone who smelled it forgot all cares and sorrows. The Prince also possessed a nightingale like no other. It could sing all the beautiful melodies

78

known throughout the world. Placing the rose and the nightingale in two handsome silver cases, he sent them to the Emperor's daughter.

The Emperor had them brought before the Princess whose eyes lit up when she saw the two cases. "Oh, I hope they're filled with rare jewels... exotic perfumes...fine china figurines," she cried. But, instead, out came the rose.

"How beautifully it is made," exclaimed the ladies of the court.

But when the Princess touched the rose, she nearly burst into tears. "Papa, please take it away," she said with distaste. "It's not *made* of anything. It's a real rose!"

"But my dear," the Emperor cautioned, "before you get too upset, let us see what is in the other case." When he opened the second present, out flew the nightingale. It sang so sweetly that, at first, everyone was overjoyed.

"Superb! Charming!" declared the ladies.

"What a magnificent music box! It looks like a real bird," the Princess said, treasuring her gift.

"But it *is* a real nightingale," said the attendants who had brought in the presents.

"Real? Well then, let it fly away!" she said in disgust and then she refused to see the Prince.

But the Prince was not so easily discouraged. Disguising himself, he smeared brown and black all over his face, pulled a hat down over his eyes, and knocked at the Emperor's door.

"Your most Gracious Highness," the Prince said humbly. I am here seeking a position within your palace. Whatever work needs to be done, I am at your service."

"Well," the Emperor muttered, "I do need a swineherd to take care of the pigs. It is not the best of positions but you will have a roof over your head and plenty of food to eat."

"I am honored," the cunning Prince answered gratefully. And he truly was thankful for now he could be near the Princess he adored.

And so the Prince became the "Imperial Swineherd." He was given a miserable little hut close to the pigsty and that was where he stayed—hardly the comforts of a royal Prince. But, he had a goal and a plan to achieve it.

The Prince labored hard at his chores. But whenever he had a spare moment, he worked on a charming little pot which he was going to give the Princess. It had little bells on the handle so that when the pot boiled the bells tinkled and played a lovely old tune:

Ah, my dearest Augustine,
All is gone, gone, gone.

One day, when the swineherd saw the Princess coming near his hut with her ladies-in-waiting, he put the pot on to boil. When the Princess heard the tinkling bells playing that tune, she stood still in astonishment. How pleased she was! That was the only piece of music she could play on the piano. "Why there is my music!" she exclaimed happily. "That swineherd must be very well educated." And so she said to one of the ladies, "Go and ask him how much the instrument costs for I *must* have it!" So one of the ladies ran into the swineherd's hut—changing her shoes first, of course.

"How much does the pot cost?" asked the lady.

"All I wish is to receive ten kisses from the Princess," he replied craftily.

"What a naughty fellow," said the enraged Princess haughtily when she heard his reply. And off she went, down the path. But she had only gone a little way when the bells tinkled so merrily that she had to stop. "How ridiculous!" said the Princess to the ladies of the court. "I will pay him. But all of you must stand around me so that no one sees us kiss!"

So the court ladies spread out their dresses and

surrounded the Princess. The swineherd, to his de-
light, got his ten kisses and the Princess got the pot.

The Prince did not let a day go by without mak-
ing something which he knew would attract the
Princess. One day he made a rattle that played all
the waltzes, jigs and polkas in the world.

"Ah, that is superb!" exclaimed the Princess as
she passed by. "Go in and ask him how much it
costs. But remember, this time no kisses."

"He wants one hundred kisses," said the lady who
had asked the swineherd, "or no rattle."

"He is impossible," said the Princess, stamping
her foot, and she marched on. But then she stopped.
"And yet, one must encourage the artisan. Ladies,
please gather round so that no one sees us." And
so they did.

Meanwhile, the Emperor came walking down the path. "What's this!" the Emperor cried just as the swineherd was taking his eighty-sixth kiss. The Emperor was so distraught that he shouted, "Get out! Get out!" to both the Princess and the swineherd. And, he told them never to return.

After the two had walked many miles, it began to rain. The Princess wept and the swineherd cursed as the water poured down.

"Oh, how unhappy I am," moaned the Princess. "If only I had married the handsome Prince who sent me the rose and the nightingale."

The swineherd slipped behind a tree, wiped the dirt from his face, and tore off his disguise. He emerged in his princely finery, looking so noble that the Princess bowed before him. She was so happy, it was like a dream come true!

But the Prince rejected her. "When I came to you as a Prince you would not have me. You didn't appreciate the magnificent rose and the beautiful nightingale, but you were willing to kiss a swineherd for a pot and a rattle. You deserve your fate!"

And with that, he went back to his own kingdom and left her behind. There was nothing for the Princess to do. So, for the remainder of her days, she sang sadly to herself:

Ah, my dearest Augustine,
All is gone, gone, gone.

It's
Perfectly
True

It happened one evening, in a hen house on the edge of town. All the hens had flown to their perches for the night. One was a lovely white-feathered bird. She laid her eggs when expected and was respectable in every way. As she nestled, she preened and plumed her feathers with her beak. She really was very pretty and very particular about keeping her feathers fluffy and clean. As she worked, a tiny feather drifted slowly to the ground.

"No matter," the hen said with a smile, "the more I plume my feathers, the more they will grow."

She had meant nothing by the words; they were just uttered thoughtlessly as she fell asleep. But the hen perched just below her took them seriously. She turned to the hen next to her and hissed, "Wake up! There is a hen—I'd rather not say her name because you know I don't tell tales—who is going to pluck out all her feathers *just* to make herself beautiful."

Even though this gossipy hen had whispered, sharp ears were listening. Just above the hen house lived a family of owls wide awake, for nighttime was really their daytime.

"Don't pay attention," said the Mother Owl. "It's none of our business if a hen wants to pluck out all of her feathers just to attract a rooster."

But the Father Owl stretched his huge wings and thought to himself, "I must go and tell our neighbors the news." And he flew off into the night.

"Whoo! Whoo!" he hooted as he swooped down over the pigeon house. "Guess what? A young hen plucked out all her feathers just to please a rooster. Foolish bird! She must be freezing to death!"

"Where?" demanded the pigeons, who perked up at once, for who could sleep when told such a story.

"It happened in the yard over there," said the owl emphatically. "I saw it with my own eyes. Not a pretty sight, to be sure, but it's perfectly true!"

Away flew the pigeons excitedly. They circled the hen yard and woke everyone. "It's true," they cooed, "there's a hen, perhaps two, who have plucked out all their feathers just to attract the rooster. They are both frozen from the cold already!"

With all the noise, the rooster was awakened. "Cock-a-doodle-do!" he crowed. "Wake up! Three hens have plucked out all their feathers and died for the love of a rooster. Tell everyone!"

"We'll tell, we'll tell," screeched the bats who heard the rooster. Night was their time, too.

And so the story went from one to another until, at last, it came back to the little white hen.

"Five hens are dead, all to make themselves more beautiful!" cried a hen. "They plucked out all their feathers just to please a rooster and then they pecked each other because of jealousy. Now they are all dead. What a shame! What a disgrace!"

"Good gracious!" said the little white hen, for she had no idea that her remark was the cause of all this trouble. She was aghast and a little angry too, to hear that hens could be so silly. She paused for a moment while preening herself and said haughtily, "Such creatures are so ridiculous. The papers should hear about this and spread the word so that no one else acts so foolishly."

And so the story was printed in the papers and everyone knew about the five foolish hens. It's all perfectly true. One small white feather, carelessly preened, can easily become five dead hens.